I'll Be There

Karl Newson   Rosalind Beardshaw

nosy crow

When **big** adventures call to us
and take us somewhere new,

I'll be there to lead the march
and **toot** my **toot** for you!

I'll Be There

Karl Newson   Rosalind Beardshaw

For Jack and Ben
– my *big* little elephants!
K.N.

To Paula and Bea, with love.
R.B. x

First published in 2022 by Nosy Crow Ltd
The Crow's Nest, 14 Baden Place,
Crosby Row, London, SE1 1YW, UK

Nosy Crow Eireann Ltd, 44 Orchard Grove,
Kenmare, Co Kerry, V93 FY22, Ireland

www.nosycrow.com

ISBN 978 1 83994 087 3 (HB)
ISBN 978 1 83994 088 0 (PB)

Nosy Crow and associated logos are trademarks and/or registered
trademarks of Nosy Crow Ltd.

Text © Karl Newson 2022
Illustrations © Rosalind Beardshaw 2022

A CIP catalogue record for this book is available from the British Library.

Printed in China

Papers used by Nosy Crow are made from wood grown in sustainable forests.

1 3 5 7 9 8 6 4 2 (HB)
1 3 5 7 9 8 6 4 2 (PB)

For all the world is yours to find — get ready to **explore!**

Go seek a world of wonders
you have never seen before.

On tricky paths, you'll know I'm there —
I'll **growl** my **growl** for you.

For some things can be hard at first,
but that's because they're new.

If they feel like **mountains** —
too impossible to dare —

just climb them slowly, step by step,
and know that I'll be there.

As rolling waves glide over us,
I'll **sing** my **song** for you.

For if you try with all your heart,
there's **nothing** you can't do.

I'll be there to help you
as you practise on your own.

Just remember this —
you'll never, **ever** be alone.

Across the waving, golden fields,
I'll **squeak** my **squeak** for you.

For some games can be played with one,
but most are **best** with two!

I'll be there to share
the little joys you find each day.

And when it's time to play your games,
I'll let you lead the way!

In every corner of the land,
I'll **roar** my **roar** for you.

And I'll be watching over you . . .

. . . till you are **roaring** too!

We'll wander home as day grows old,
but when the sunbeams soar,

you know that I'll be there
to go **adventuring** once more.

To starlit skies and back again,
I'll **hoot** my **hoot** for you!

We'll share our secret wishes,
and I'll wish your dreams come true.

And if the dark feels just **too** dark,
the **moon** will be our light.

I'll be there to keep you safe . . .

. . . all through the deepest night.

For you can make the world light up with just the smallest smile.

And I'll be there to see you shine
and love you all the while.

Yes, I'll be there to see you shine
and love you all the while.